CAPTAIN SAWYER AND THE GOLDEN STATUE OF AURORA

TALISHA ANTONIO

Illustrated by
WARREN K MEZA

First published by RMPublishers Ltd, 2025

Copyright © 2025 by Talisha Antonio

Illustrations by Talisha Antonio and Warren K Meza

A CIP catalogue of this book is available from the British Library.

ISBN: 978-1-0683808-2-2

2nd Edition

I dedicate this book to my children Dean, Dante, Saana and Ashanti Chauke.

To my nieces Reina Antonio, Ruvarashe Chauke, Amira Scholtz, Nombeko Ndou, Kimberly Moyo, Lesedi Moyo, Angel Rose Wilcox, Kimberly Meza, Shana Sangare, Shanice Sangare, Keren Sithole, Monica, Rute and Esther Manico.

To my nephews Yelisey Antonio, Ilidio Johachim Antonio, Uzayr Scholtz, Inaam Adam-Shaik , Zaydaan Abdullah, Thabani Chauke, Liam Meza, Shane Meza, Owen Shamu, Christian Moyo, Michael Moyo, Jadon Moyo, Ngoni Ndou, Tafara Ndou, Thembalami Ndou, Jayden Sangare, Jayden Mabhena, Joshua Mabhena, Jacob Mabhena. Creflo (aka C K) Sithole.

To my baby cousins Tawananyasha (aka T.J) and Kupakwashe Myles Meza. Natasha Chimanikire, Ralph Chisuko, Deyasha, Daniella and Allicious Antonio.

You all inspire me to be more and to do better. I love you all. My precious gifts from God.

ACKNOWLEDGMENTS

Firstly, I would like to thank God my Father, Creator, Provider and Protector. I thank You, Lord, for all my blessings and for giving me so many Gifts, Talents, creativity and abilities. In the name of **Yeshua**, I give **you** all the glory.

To my mother Fairesi Sinclair, I love and appreciate you. My real-life superhero.

To my cousin and creative partner, Warren (Kudzi) Meza. Thank you for always believing in me and bringing it to life through your sketches. I love you always.

To my friend and sister Sunday Morgan (Voga) thank you for believing in me and having my back. Thank you for coming to my rescue. I love and appreciate you.

To my friends/sisters, Maria Nascimento, Sara Francisco and Marcia T Chigumira Chauke, I love you all so much, thank you for believing, encouraging and motivating me.

Lindiwe Solomon, thank you for always taking the time to go through my projects and advising me on how to make the necessary changes that were needed.

To my friend and sister Dr Naar Mercy Holloway, thank you for taking the time to go through my work and for all your encouragement.

To my accountability partner and fellow author and

creative, Sister Bethia aka Melanie Steadman. Thank you for helping make this second edition possible.

To Rudo Muchoko, thank you for the PAWAR conference. This conference helped me realise that anything to do with my gift of writing was possible. Thank you for creating an amazing platform, RMPublishers, a place in which we can showcase our God-given gifts and talents.

CHAPTER ONE

Captain Jack Sawyer was a tall, dark-haired and well-mannered man. His humility enabled him to respectfully walk into the King's quarters, bowing quickly, showing his respect as he stood in the King's presence. King Marca III nodded and made a hand gesture. Jack nodded back and sat in front of the King while he kept pacing up and down, which made Jack feel a bit uneasy.

The King was very fair-minded, wise and humble. He ruled and served his people just as his forefathers had done for generations. King Marca was married to the beautiful princess of the Merina. He had two sons, Mowan and Marca IV, and two beautiful daughters, Merina, who was named after her mother's land and Maya, who was the youngest of his children. The king loved all his children and loved his land.

Jack cleared his throat and spoke, "Your majesty, you requested to see me, Sire?" The King stopped. Looking at Jack, he took a deep breath and sat down slowly. He cleared his throat and said,

"Jack, I have a mission for you. It is a very urgent mission and it will require your full attention."

Jack adjusted himself slightly in the chair, swallowed and whilst maintaining eye contact with the King, Jack responded,

"I am at your service, your majesty."

Captain Jack Sawyer was well known across the seven seas of Ventura and Tashi. He had a very good reputation that spoke of his bravery, kindness and fierceness in battle. He was the perfect gentleman and a great soldier that loyally served the King and his kingdom.

Jack was the last-born child of Ryan and Isabella Sawyer. He grew up on a farm with four other siblings; two sisters, Joan and Josephine and two older brothers, Jason and Joseph. Jack's great-grandparents had immigrated to the land of Aurora in search of a better life and new beginnings. Jack's great-grandfather James Sawyer joined the army, trained, worked hard and served loyally, whilst Jack's grandmother Amina stayed home and looked after the children. Jack's grand-father Samuel also served, but he served in the Royal Navy. Ryan, Jack's father met Isabella, Jack's mother in Aurora whilst he was serving as a soldier in the King's army. Isabella worked as an army nurse and she was also in service under the King. They both fell in love, married and had their children whilst still in service. It was after they had completed their 20 years of service that they retired to live on a farm they had purchased with their savings.

Jack, being the youngest, spent most of his younger years on the farm. He enjoyed helping his parents with the day-to-day duties of the farm and, like his siblings, he was very intelligent, gifted and talented. Jack excelled in academic and sporting activities. His parents raised him and his siblings in a way that taught them to be humble, respectful and empathetic to others, they also encouraged them to have confidence, purpose, values and to be disciplined. Jack's family had a strong Christian background, which was also the faith of the whole Kingdom of Aurora.

Jack had always wanted to serve like his father, grandfather and great grandfather before him in the King's army and navy. Jack was born to serve as a soldier, unlike his siblings who went on to pursue careers in politics, medicine, law and teaching. Jack joined the King's Navy where he served from junior ranks and worked his way up to become a Captain of his own ship, the ship Zahra. The ship was named after the King's mother, Queen Zahra.

Captain Jack Sawyer

CHAPTER TWO

Jack, having received the orders from the King, left the palace and made his way to where his ship was docked. It was a bright and sunny day and there was not a single cloud in the sky. The sea looked calm, which made Jack smile. As he stepped onto the ship, all the men stopped what they were doing, and stood at attention as a sign of respect for their captain. The ship's second in command, Paddy, walked towards Captain Jack and met him on the deck. He saluted and Jack did the same. Jack then shouted to his men, "At ease men!"

The men continued with what they had been doing before the captain had come on board. Jack and Paddy walked down into the captain's office. Jack sat down, took a deep breath in and exhaled. He signaled for Paddy Wolfe to take a seat. Paddy pulled a chair out and sat down. He had never seen the captain like this, he was not sure whether the captain was angry, anxious or confused. This was the first time Paddy could not read the captain or figure out what he was thinking. He too became worried as he waited on what news the captain had from the King.

Jack closed his eyes and rested his face in his hands. He was not sure what to make of the King's new orders, but being the man he was, he was going to do everything in his power to make sure he followed the orders. He was not sure how the men would react, but they too would have to follow the orders that had been given to them.

Jack lifted his head and stood up, and looked out at the sea. He could sense Paddy's discomfort, so he turned and looked at his colleague. Jack smiled which made Paddy relax and sigh. He then cleared his throat and said to Paddy, "I have our new orders Paddy, and I don't know what to make of them."

Captain Sawyer looking out at the sea

Paddy sat back in his chair and braced himself ready to hear what the new orders were. Jack licked his dry lips, cleared his throat and then he sat back down in his chair behind his desk. He looked down at the paper lying on his desk, not sure of how to tell his colleague what their next mission was. Jack pursed his lips and looked up at Paddy, making eye contact. Paddy saw the look of regret in the captain's eyes and leaned forward, anticipating what the captain's next words were going to be. Paddy could hear his own heart pounding in his chest. He looked at Jack and interrupted him.

"Jack, is everything okay? Are you going to take me out of my misery?"

The captain leaned forward and shook his head as if wanting to say no. Instead he opened his mouth to speak but before he could say anything he was interrupted by a knock at the door. Both men turned to look at the door and then looked at each other.

"Come in!" they both shouted.

The door swung open and four of Jack's lieutenants walked in. They lined up behind Paddy and stood at attention whilst saluting both Captain Jack and Paddy, who exchanged looks before they both started laughing.

The lieutenants looked at each other in confusion and then turned to look at the captain and Paddy. Jack still laughing said,

"Are you telling me that you men could not wait a few more minutes to find out what our new orders were?"

The men exchanged looks and then one of them stepped forward ready to address the captain.

The Captain led a crew of fifty-four men and each one of them served on the ship with honor, loyalty and dedication. They lived and fought together on the ship and the land like a family. They trusted their Captain and he trusted each one of his men with his life. Jack had five deputies who were his second in command, including Paddy Wolfe, also known as Aaron. Aaron loved wolves, so this was how he earned his nickname. The other four lieutenants were Michael, Keith,

Samuel and Keanu. They all worked together to ensure the smooth running of the ship. They all helped to maintain order, harmony and when needed, they were good at keeping the men focused and motivated.

Paddy Wolfe had served alongside the captain for as long as both he and the captain had served under the King. Paddy and Jack had met as young lads and trained up together. It was as if they were destined to meet and serve on the same ship. Paddy had been given several opportunities to captain his ship, but he had declined each time as he wanted to remain by his friend's side. He always felt the time was not right for him to leave his friend and the ship, Zahra, besides he felt they made a great team.

Paddy had a wife, Zoya, and two children - Jonah and Sarah. Paddy had given up trying to fix his friend up with some of his wife's friends who all wanted to be seen at the great Captain's side.

Lieutenant Samuel, the one who had stepped forward to respond to the captain's question, had only served under one captain and on one ship, the ship Zahra, which was under Captain Jack Sawyer. Although he did not have as much experience as the two men, Paddy and Jack, he had served longer and was more experienced than the other lieutenants.

Samuel was married to one of Aurora's well-known surgeons, Dr. Sandra Rice. Lieutenant Keith was single and lived with his parents in a small town in Aurora. Keith was one of the youngest serving lieutenants in the King's army and just like Captain Jack, he was working his way up the ranks. He hoped one day to oversee his ship and lead a crew of men just like his Captain.

Keith had always admired the captain and once he had been allowed to serve under the great captain. He worked hard at everything he was assigned to do, which gained him recognition from the great captain who promoted him and moved him up the ranks to the rank where he was now. Keith loved being a Lieutenant. It allowed him to work close to the captain, which allowed him to learn everything he could from the captain as he prepared to move up to the role of captain of his ship.

Lieutenant Michael was single. He came from a family of serving men, his great-grandfather, grandfather, father, uncles, cousins and brothers all served in the king's army or navy and just like his colleague Lieutenant Keith, Michael worked hard and moved up the ranks. He too hoped to lead his crew but for now he was happy where he was. Serving was all he knew to do. Lieutenant Keanu had just married the love of his life, his high school sweetheart and best friend, Anashe, who worked as a teacher.

Keanu was just like his colleagues; he was a hardworking and dedicated man who served with honor. He hoped to start a family with his wife, and unlike his colleagues, he hoped he would be stationed on land. He had put a request in and was waiting for his new assignment, if it was approved. He hoped to move up the ranks on land where he would be able to stay with his newly wed wife.

Lieutenant Samuel wiped his brow and cleared his throat. He answered the captain's question.

"Captain, we could not help but notice the look on your face when you boarded, sir."

"Aha, you see..." said Paddy as he turned to look at the Captain. "You got them worried too".

Jack turned and looked out at the sea again. The team helped him to run the ship and to keep the peace in the land of Aurora. They also helped to protect the borders of their beautiful kingdom.

Jack had always served the king without question and he was not going to start now. He wasn't sure of what to make of this new mission, but one way or the other he was going to have to let his men know what was going on. He wasn't sure how they were going to react, but he knew just like him, they were going to follow the orders given to them by the king.

Paddy looked out at the sea too and could not help wondering what it was that had got his friend to behave in such a strange manner. Paddy began to tap his fingers impatiently and then he cleared his throat. Jack could hear the tapping, which quickly brought him back to reality. Jack looked at all five men and then he started to laugh quietly. He admired and respected each one of them and could not help but to think how they all would be baffled by this new assignment. He stopped laughing because he could see that Paddy was beginning to lose his patience. Jack had known his friend for a long time, so he was quick to recognize that Paddy was beginning to slowly lose his patience.

The captain quickly stood up and removed his jacket as he was beginning to feel hot. He wiped his brow and cleared his throat for the last time. He then looked at the men and Paddy stood up and walked towards the lieutenants. He went and stood beside them ready to hear whatever the captain was going to say. Jack waited for Paddy and then began to speak.

"The King's orders are to escort his daughter Princess Maya and her friends to the Kemi Islands." Paddy and the

Lieutenants exchanged looks and looked at the captain in confusion. Only Paddy could ask the captain,

"We have been asked to do what?"

Jack looked at his men and smiled. He told them again, "The king has assigned us to escort Princess Maya and her friends to the Kemi Islands. We are to start preparing immediately so we can leave first thing tomorrow. Please brief the men and prepare the ship. We will be gone for a few weeks. For those who need to say their goodbyes, please do so and return for duty early tomorrow morning.

The four lieutenants saluted the captain and left. As soon as they shut the door, Paddy and Jack burst out laughing. Jack turned to ask Paddy,

"Did you see the look on their faces?" Jack laughed.

"Did you see the look on your face too, Paddy? The look on your face was of utter shock?"

Paddy stopped laughing and said to the Captain,

"Jack, you too were in shock, what kind of a mission is this? How are we the crew of the great Ship Zahra supposed to be babysitting the princess and her friends?"

They both stopped to think about how it all sounded. Then they both burst out laughing. Jack quickly said to Paddy,

"You need to get the lieutenants to assign a team to look after the princess and her friends".

Paddy responded quickly,

"Yes sir. We don't want them getting in the way of our important mission sir."

The men both looked at each other and laughed again.

JACK REMEMBERED his first encounter with the beautiful princess. It was at a ball that the king had thrown. Jack did not like attending these things, but he had no choice as it was a requirement for him and his men to attend. He remembered seeing the beautiful princess who was tall and beautiful. He had struggled to focus on what was going on around him and chose to leave the event early. He had made up an excuse that he had some paperwork to finish, but the real reason had been that he had been caught off guard and was not used to feeling the way he felt each time the princess looked at him.

And every time she had smiled, he had felt a little tug at his heart. He had crossed paths with the princess on several occasions but had done his best to avoid her. He liked to be in control, focused so he made sure after each greeting, he would disappear into the crowd and he kept himself occupied. He had encounters with a lot of women who had gone out of their way to try and get his attention, which they had never received, but this time was different. The princess had him mesmerized and she had done nothing whatsoever to get his attention.

This was why he could not be the one to watch over her, assigning crew members was the best move, besides he thought he didn't have the patience to deal with the rich and privileged people. She probably was a very spoilt little princess. "Yes," he thought and whispered to himself, "I will keep my distance. It is probably for the best."

Captain Sawyer giving his deputy Paddy
Wolfe instructions

CHAPTER THREE

Maya walked into her father's office and could not hide her excitement. She had been patiently waiting for her father to summon her to his office. It had been two weeks since she had asked for his permission to go to the Kemi Islands with her friends. Her father had not been keen about her leaving the kingdom.

Maya had managed to convince the queen of how the trip would benefit the kingdom, who in turn had managed to talk to the king on Maya's behalf. Maya had no doubt it was going to happen. She was now ever so certain because she had been in the study a few doors away from her father's office when she heard the maidens whisper about the captain's arrival. Maya couldn't help but smile because she too often had secret quiet conversations about the captain with her friends.

Who did not know of the great Captain Jack Sawyer? Maya knew that her father was concerned for her safety and that would be the only reason the captain would be summoned at such short notice to the Palace. Maya could feel her heart beating against her chest. She curtsied and waited for her father to nod as he always did, but this time when he did there was no smile on his face. Maya's excitement quickly turned into fear and disappointment. She was no longer sure of what her father was going to say because he had that serious look on his face. It was the same look he gave her whenever she had done something wrong and was in trouble.

Maya slowly sat down and looked down at her hands in her lap that were shaking. She looked up at her father who was still wearing a serious look on his face. She swallowed and slowly released the breath she had been holding in from the moment she had seen the look on her father's face. Was she in trouble? Maya could not help but feel like she was a little girl again. She always used to get into trouble for being mischievous when she was younger, but being the youngest, she always got told off, but she was never smacked or punished.

The king could see how troubled his daughter was. She had looked so excited when she had skipped into his office. He was happy to see her but needed her to understand the seriousness and the importance of the situation. The journey she was about to take away from the safety of her home. He could not believe how quickly time had passed; it was just the other day he had held her in his arms as a baby. Now here he was looking at his little girl who was not so little anymore. He felt sad because he had always known this day would come.

Maya had grown up to be just like him. He knew the day would come when she would want to venture out of the kingdom. King Marca closed his eyes and put his hand on his chest. He could not believe he was going to allow his baby girl to leave the kingdom and venture out there without him or her mother or older siblings. King Marca sighed and opened his eyes and looked at his little princess. Maya fidgeted a little in her chair. She could not imagine what was going on in her father's head. She remembered her two older sisters telling her it would never happen. Her father would not let her leave the kingdom. Maya looked down again, and this time she started to pray silently. She kept thinking to herself, "This is for a good cause, this is for a good cause, Oh Lord please let it be a yes, Oh God please."

The King cleared his throat and started speaking, but Maya could not hear a thing because of the thudding of her heart in her ears. She quickly snapped out of it and asked her father.

"I beg your pardon Father; please could you repeat what you just said?"

The king, a little annoyed, replied, "I hope you understand the seriousness of this, Maya. It is with a heavy heart that I am allowing you to go to the Kemi Islands with your friends."

Maya squealed and jumped out of her chair. Just for a moment she forgot where she was and started dancing. Maya was so excited she began to laugh and jump up and down with joy. The king cleared his throat and it was then that she remembered where she was. She turned and looked at her father who did not look impressed at all. Maya blushed and smiled at her father, stopped and then she sat down. The king was a little annoyed but had loved seeing his daughter happy, so he had sat back and watched her jump up and down with excitement. The King raised his pointer figure and wagged it at his daughter. Maya quickly sits back in her seat, unable to contain herself. She leaned forward and waited to listen to what else her father had to say. The king shook his head and smiled.

"Listen Maya, I have assigned Captain Sawyer and his men to take you to the islands and I am expecting nothing but the best behavior from you and your friends, do you hear?"

The princess nodded her head, got out of her chair and ran to hug her father.

"I won't let you down father."

The king shrugged and held his daughter at arm's length, he looked straight into her eyes and then he said to her,

"I want you to look me in the eyes and I want to hear you say it Maya"

"I promise you father, I will be on my best behavior. I will listen to everything that the captain and his men say, and we will be on our best behavior."

The king considered what his daughter was saying as he looked into her eyes and saw how sincere she was. He cuddled her and said,

"Okay, you can tell your friends the news and get yourselves ready because you are leaving first thing in the morning. Do not keep the captain and his men waiting."

"Yes father," the princess curtsied her way out of the King's office, "Thank you so much father."

The princess hugging her Father, the King

CHAPTER FOUR

Maya had grown into a very tall and beautiful young woman, she had big brown eyes, beautiful, smooth, radiant dark brown skin and long beautiful curly brown hair. **With her** smile she always used to charm her father to get whatever she wanted and everyone else in the household, this included her big brothers, the two princes. Princess Maya wanted to have an ordinary life, so she tried to fit in and asked not to be treated like royalty, which was very difficult because everyone knew who she was. Maya was very intelligent, humble and selfless. She worked with orphaned children and served the people of her father's kingdom alongside her parents and siblings.

She loved learning new things and she was very creative. She wanted to learn the Paya, which was a special art. She knew if she learnt this, she would teach it to the younger women in the kingdom. This new skill would allow the women to make clothes, jewellery, bags and other accessories, which they could sell in different lands. This would allow them to develop a skill they could pass down for generations.

Maya ran through the palace, hugging everyone she crossed paths with, telling them the great news. She was finally going on the trip. She was finally going to do something that mattered. She sent word to her friends to prepare themselves to leave the next day. She was so excited and when her sister heard the news, she went to help her prepare for her journey.

As the maids, Maya and her sister princess Merina were packing and talking about the captain, the ship and the trip, Maya could not help but remember the first time she had seen the captain at the great ball held to honor her brother's graduation. Prince Mowan had finished his studies with distinctions and had made his parents proud. It was on this day that she had seen the captain. They had been briefly introduced but she had not had an opportunity to have any further conversations with him as he had been swept away by her brothers who wanted to introduce him to their friends.

She had felt her heart melt when he had taken her hand and kissed it, she knew this was how all the men in the kingdom greeted the maidens when they were first introduced, but she felt there was more to it and it meant something to both of them. She had declined all the advances from the young princes at the ball and had turned down every offer to dance with them in hopes that the Captain would come and ask her to dance. This did not happen, which had made her sad, but Maya was happy because the captain had not danced with anyone else at all.

As she folded her clothes, she smiled to herself and remembered that as the captain was leaving, he turned and looked around the room and when their eyes locked, she felt butterflies in her stomach. He had smiled at her and her heart had skipped a beat. He nodded, turned and left the ball. Maya had seen him on several occasions afterwards, but he was always busy or preoccupied. It seemed as if he was avoiding her. The princess frowned, and her sister noticed.

"Maya, what is wrong, why are you not happy?" asked princess Merina.

"Nothing" responded Maya.

"Little sister, what is going on in that little head of yours?"

Maya slowly sat down and started to get a sinking feeling. She turned and looked at her sister, asking, "What if he doesn't like me?"

"What if who doesn't like you?" she asked

"The Captain" replies Maya, "Captain Jack Sawyer"

Princess Merina sat down next to her sister, looking at her and smiled because she too could remember exactly how she had felt when she had met her love. She also had the same look on her face. Princess Merina hugged her little sister and reassured her that it would all work out. All she had to do was put it in God's hands.

THE FOLLOWING MORNING, the princess woke up early and prepared herself to leave, her two friends, Amara and Skye, came racing into her room. They all screamed and hugged each other, excited and speaking at the same time. Amara and Skye noticed Princess Merina sitting in the room, so they both stopped and curtsied, so Princess Merina shook her head and said,

"I don't know why you two insist on doing that, you both are part of the family." She turned and hugged her sister princess Maya and said to her, "I am going to miss you little sister." She turned and looked at Amara and Skye and said, "I will also miss you two." Maya smiled at her sister and responded, "I am going to miss you too." Princess Merina looked at the three ladies in front of her and said, "I pray that you will have a safe trip and we pray God brings you all back home safely" and they all responded. "Amen."

The queen walked in and they all curtsied. The queen rolled her eyes and said to them, "Oh, stop it now, come on here and hug me. I pray for God's protection over each one of you."

The queen asked the girls to hold hands and then she said a prayer for a safe journey and their safe return. They were all in agreement and they listened to the queen's advice.

Maya was still worried about meeting the captain. She prayed that this was the opportunity that she had been hoping for. Somehow God had made it possible for an opportunity like this to occur. She was finally going to be able to get to know the captain. She had prayed that her father would allow her to go on a journey like this but had never thought her father would arrange it the way he had. She was nervous and excited too.

"Maya!" the Queen called.

"Yes mum," the princess responded.

"It is time." The queen exchanged looks with her daughter and the girls made their way to the court where the king and his men were waiting for them to escort them to the ship.

As they drew closer to the harbor, Maya gripped her sister's hand. Princess Merina leaned in and whispered, "All is well, Maya, it is going to be okay." Maya nodded and took a deep breath, exhaling slowly. She felt very nervous and was struggling to stay calm. She saw the ship and her heart began to race again. She tightened her grip on her sister's hand and Merina embraced and kissed her on the forehead.

They arrived and disembarked, and the royal family walked towards the ship where all the crew members were waiting to greet them. Captain Jack and his deputy, Paddy, and the four lieutenants waited patiently as the royal family approached. They all bowed as a sign of respect. The King approached the captain and shook his hand. The king addressed the captain and his men,

"I would like to thank you once again for your continued service, and I trust that you will all do everything in your power to ensure the safety of my daughter and her friends."

"Yes, your highness, they are in safe hands and we will ensure that they are safe at all times, sir. You have my word." The Captain responded.

The King said a prayer for everyone on the ship and spoke a blessing over his daughter, her friends, the crew and everyone who was staying behind, he bade them farewell.

Jack knew this was the first time they had been given such a mission, but no matter how strange or different it seemed, he was going to make sure it worked out perfectly. When the king and the rest of the royals had left and returned to the palace, Jack introduced the princess and her friends to the crew, because he did not know how to handle the way he felt when he was around the princess. Jack quickly excused himself and left the rest to Paddy, who took Princess Maya, her friends and her entourage to a side room where he told them a few housekeeping rules and instructed them on a few emergency procedures, he then led them to their quarters. After showing them to their rooms, Paddy quickly excused himself and left the princess and her friends in the Lieutenant's care. The princess did not understand why the Captain had not stayed longer and given them a tour of his ship; she was a little confused but did not think much of it. The rest of the princess's entourage settled in and the ship set sail.

The princess and her friends arrive on the ship

CHAPTER FIVE

The Princess walked onto the deck and looked up at the sky. They had been sailing for two weeks now, and the weather had been good. The sky was clear and although the sun shone bright in the sky, there was a cool breeze that made it bearable to be in the heat. The princess breathed in the fresh air and slowly exhaled. She couldn't help but feel very sad. She had not seen the captain for days, and she somehow felt he was avoiding her, but could not understand why? Maya closed her eyes and said a silent prayer. She knew she had to focus on the purpose of the trip. It was for a good cause and she did not intend to fail on her quest.

Maya joined her friends who had all settled in quite well on the ship and were enjoying the attention they were receiving from the two younger lieutenants. Maya smiled to herself and thought, at least her friends had found love. On the bridge, Jack stood watching the princess and her companions. He had started to hear more about the humble princess who was on board his ship and in his care.

The crew would not stop talking about the princess and her companions, which made Jack grow very fond and curious about the beautiful princess. He questioned himself whether he had judged her unfairly. Jack closed his eyes and shook his head. He did not have any idea how he was going to handle any awkward situation, so he found it easier to retreat.

Paddy, who had been standing next to him because he had been curious to see what had taken his friend's attention, cleared his throat. This broke Jack's chain of thoughts as he hadn't realized Paddy had been standing next to him. He also did not know how long he had been there. Paddy smiled at Jack and said, "So, Captain, when are you going to stop hiding and finally sit down and get to know the beautiful princess?"

Jack rolled his eyes at Paddy and looked away. He then whispered, "I am not hiding..." Paddy raised his brow at him and chuckled,

"Of course you're not hiding! I'm not stupid, Jack, I can see what's going on."

Jack looked at his friend and asked, "What's going on?"

Paddy responded, a little annoyed, "You had better put the princess out of her misery. Go on and have a conversation with the lady, better yet, let us have a banquet in honor of our guests, it is not every day we get to have such precious cargo on board."

"Cargo?" asked Jack

"I mean precious guests" Paddy laughed, "I expect to see you all dressed up and in the dining hall with everyone else at eighteen hundred hours. Don't make me send a search party out, I will get them to drag you down to the mess hall if I have to, you know I will."

Jack nodded his head and excused himself. He knew his friend would do it. He went to prepare himself for the night ahead. He was finally going to sit down and have a conversation with the first woman he had met who had managed to get under his skin. Jack laughed as he looked for something to wear. Paddy was still meddling just like his parents did, trying to get him to settle down and this time the only difference was that he didn't mind at all. He was looking forward to this event, he was excited.

When the princess and her friends heard about the special banquet being held in their honor, they were very thrilled. They went off to prepare for the event. The princess's friends were both beautiful, smart, intelligent and humble ladies from very wealthy families. They enjoyed attending events and shared the same interest as their friend, Princess Maya.

As they walked away, Maya hesitated a little as she was not sure of what to make of the news. She looked at Paddy who was smiling at her, then she curtsied and slowly turned and walked away to prepare for the evening. She hoped the captain would be present and she would finally get to sit and talk to him. She couldn't help but feel hopeful.

The princess walks away to prepare for the evening

THE CAPTAIN WALKED in and all the men stood up to salute him. He saluted back and they all waited for him to take his seat. The men all sat down after the captain had sat down and continued with their conversations, everyone happy and excited.

Paddy looked over at his friend and smiled. Jack noticed and asked, "What is it, Paddy?" The Lieutenants exchanged looks and smiled as they all waited for Paddy's response. Paddy slapped his friend's shoulder and said to him,

"You clean up very well captain!"

They all laughed before a sudden silence fell in the entire room. Jack and Paddy turned to see the three beautiful women walk in. The men all stood up and waited for the princess and her two friends to get to their seats and they all sat down. A prayer was said, and then the food was served. The banquette allowed the Captain to get to know these beautiful women whom the crew had been buzzing about.

When they arrived at the Kemi Islands, the captain

participated in everything that was going on. His two lieutenants, Keith and Michael, had fallen head over heels in love with the princess's friends Skye and Amara. Captain Jack and Princess Maya had fallen deeply in love. They soon became inseparable. Skye and Amara both came from very wealthy families. Skye's father was the owner of the Aurora Palace department stores and Amara's Father was the owner of the five-star Aurora Palace hotels. Their fathers had been friends with the king from their early childhood and their friendship had transferred to their children who had grown up, side by side.

The trip had been amazing because these men would never have had the opportunity to meet and to know these young women because of their high status. This was the first time the captain and his men had been given such a mission that changed their lives in such a way. The trip seemed too short even though they had been away for weeks. They were all excited to return and share what they had learned and for the very first time in his life, Jack had good news for his parents.

This news was going to stop them from trying to set him up with different young women, his parents had been pressuring him to settle down, and for the very first time he felt he had met the love of his life. The news of the captain and the princess's romance spread fast. It had the whole kingdom buzzing; the staff in the palace was buzzing. They were all happy that the youngest of the royal family had finally found love, they were all excited because this meant there would be another royal wedding soon.

There was only one member of staff who was not happy and that was the King's Aid, Jean Paul. Jean Paul could not believe what was happening. He kept pacing up and down in his private office. He was fuming, huffing and puffing. He grabbed the glass he had been drinking his whisky from and slammed it against the wall. He could not imagine how he had missed the signs. If he had known something was brewing between the princess and the captain, he would have found a way to get on that ship to the Kemi Islands.

———

JEAN PAUL THREW himself onto the chair and put his head in his hands. He had been trying his best to woo the princess. He had done everything he could. He had approached her on several occasions and at different events, but she did not seem moved by his gestures. He was always first in line to ask her to dance, but she had always turned him down, but because she would not dance with anyone else, he had thought nothing of it. She always smiled and was very respectful towards him, so he thought he had a chance. He did not realise that Captain Sawyer had had his eyes set on the Princess and he had never seen them together, so he had not been suspicious of them at all.

He made a fist and banged it on his desk. He had to come up with a plan. He needed to win the princess over, and he was going to do everything in his power to. Jean Paul wanted the princess's hand in marriage, and it was not because he was in love with the princess, it was for his own selfish reasons. He was not going to stop until she was his and until he got his way. The captain was not going to succeed in taking what was his, never.

So, when he was not at the King's side, Jean Paul would be sifting through the kingdom's records, history and laws. He needed something he could use. He spent hours sifting through paperwork looking for ideas and a way he could come up with a plan that would help him get what he wanted. One night, whilst he was going through the records, Jean Paul was ready to give up, when he came across something that caught his eye.

He read the text repeatedly, grabbed a paper and pen and started taking notes. By the time Jean Paul reported for work, he knew exactly what he was going to do. He had taken over from his father who had served the King loyally as his aid. When his father fell ill, he was forced by his family to quit his studies, and because he was the oldest son, he had to take over from where his father had left off. Jean Paul did as he was instructed but grew bitter and jealous of the king and his family. He knew it was the duty of his family to continue as an aid to the royal dynasty but felt this was not what he had wanted to do.

He wanted to go into politics, have money and power, unlike his father, whom he saw as a mere servant to the king. He had grown up in the palace and played alongside the two princes and had wished he was a prince too as he had seen the attention and treatment they received. The two princes had tried to make him feel like a part of the family, but he resented them and grew to hate the fact that he too would be an aid to one of them when they took over as King.

He had tried to convince his father to let him go and follow his ambition but to no avail. He had failed to sway his father from the call of duty. He had persuaded his father to let him pursue his studies, in which he hoped, whilst working as a politician, he would be able to influence and change the rules regarding the traditions and laws. He thought he would be able to find a way out of his family's obligations to the royal family.

Sadly, Jean Paul's father, Ramus, fell ill, and he had no choice but to take over his father's duties.

Whilst working as the king's aid, he realized that he could marry into the royal family because the King only cared about his children's happiness and did not worry much about them marrying royalty if their children were in love with people who were honest, honorable, humble and selfless. Jean Paul wanted to be served, he was royalty, so he had set his eyes on Princess Maya.

He felt she was easier to manipulate because he thought she was naïve, and he could not believe she did not want to be treated like royalty. He did not have much respect for her, but his ambition was to become a member of the royal family instead of a servant, so he set his plan in motion. Jean Paul approached the King and showed him what he had discovered in the records he had been going through.

"Your Majesty, for someone like the captain to marry one of your daughters, he would have to earn his place in your family,"

The king quietly responded,

"Oh Jean, that is complete and utter rubbish. The kingdom stopped following those old traditions decades ago."

Jean-Paul smiled and bowed to the king, "Sire, it is only for you and your family I am looking out for, you know I am very fond of the princess and only want what is best for her."

The King walked towards the window and looked out at the courtyard. He loved all his children and only wanted the best for them. He knew this was going to break his daughter's heart. Jean Paul had put him in a very difficult situation by approaching the elders first, there was no way he could not follow the laws his forefathers had followed. He was annoyed and turned to look at Jean-Paul. He couldn't even stand the sight of him. Instead of talking to him, he used his hand to dismiss him. As soon as he was alone, he sat down and inhaled heavily. He had seen how Jean-Paul had been watching his daughter, but he didn't realize he would stoop this low to get what he wanted.

The king was not even sure what it was, all he knew was that he did not trust Jean Paul, he had always had a bad feeling about him, but he knew one way or the other the truth would be revealed. He could not trust his aid, He never did, he had the wrong attitude for the job. If it wasn't for the respect he had for Jean-Paul's father, he would have refused to have him as his aid.

Jean-Paul couldn't help but smile to himself as he walked out of the king's office. He kept thinking of how angry the king looked. He knew the king had no choice but to do as he had suggested, he had given him no choice. He could not wait to see his plan unfolding, he knew it couldn't fail, he had covered all his bases and had contacted the people he was going to use to make his plan succeed. He stopped and began laughing. He even had the King doing his bidding. Jean-Paul continued to smile as he walked back into his office, he was finally going to get rid of the captain once and for all.

Jean-Paul in his office searching through the
Kingdom's records

CHAPTER SIX

Jack received his new orders. He sat down, his heart sinking. How could this be happening now? How was he going to break the news to his men? This was going to be impossible, the Golden statue of Aurora. Jack closed his eyes and started to pray, this was going to be a very difficult mission, a dangerous one. A mission that he and his men could not return from. He lifted his head when he heard a knock at the door, Paddy walked in. The smile on Paddy's face slowly faded away when he saw the look on Jack's face.

"What is it Jack? What is the new mission?"

"The Golden Statue of Aurora."

"The what?" Paddy asked the captain again...

"Paddy, the Golden Statue of Aurora. We need to round up the men because the orders are for us to leave by the end of the week, and that is in two days," the captain said.

Paddy and Jack sat in silence, they could not believe this

was happening to them, no ship had been sent in search of this statue and treasure for ages.

The Golden Statue of Aurora went missing after it had been stolen from the palace together with some of the kingdom's treasure. It had been missing for decades, there had been so many rumors of who had stolen it. Many had gone in search of it, and some had returned empty-handed, and some had not returned at all. The only thing that existed were portraits and pictures in library books and museums.

The Golden Statue was a silhouette of the beautiful princess Neesa who was one of King Marca's ancestors. It had been carved from pure gold and given to her by a royal prince from the land of the Meza who had asked for her hand in marriage. Their union had brought peace to both lands and the statue was a reminder of this. Legend had it that it was hidden on the island of skulls, across the four deadly seas of North Kaya, which were the only seas Captain Sawyer and his crew had never dared to cross.

The Captain had been shown the documents that Jean Paul had presented to the king and he understood the importance of the mission. Jack had not thought of setting sail for months because he had been enjoying his time with the princess. It was the night before Captain Sawyer was due to depart to find the kingdom's long-lost treasure - the Golden Statue of Aurora. He was restless, on edge, and had never felt this way before about a mission and for the first time he did not look forward to leaving.

Jack had so many questions running through his mind. Would the journey be safe? Would they meet obstacles on the way? He had just found true love and had finally fallen in love.

What about his lovely, beautiful princess? Jack shuddered at the thought of not ever seeing her. He could not forget the look on her face when he had told her that he had to leave. The princess was so distraught that he had struggled to calm her down. He knew no matter what they encountered, he had to return. He knew of the many captains who had been tasked to search for the statue and had failed to return the statue to its rightful place. If the treasure was out there, he knew he had the best crew around, they would find it.

Jack had been carrying around a ring in his pocket and had been working up the courage to ask the king for his daughter's hand in marriage. He sat at the dinner table with both his parents and siblings and their families. They were all very quiet and he could see the sadness in their eyes. He saw the tears in his mother's eyes and knew they were all thinking the same thoughts he had been thinking. His father stood up and instructed them all to bow their heads to pray. He covered his family with a prayer for hope, protection and victory over all his family and especially Jack, and all the men that served under him.

As Jack left his parents' house, he felt hopeful. Being with his family and listening to his father's prayers reminded him that he had a lot to look forward to and a bright future when he returned from his mission.

Jack breathed in the cool night air and he rode to the castle, together with his brothers. He thought of what he had experienced over the past few months. He had become a changed man. He thanked God for everything he had in his life and he prayed that God would protect him and his crew. He especially asked God to protect them all and he asked for guidance. He was going to return to the Kingdom of Aurora safely, together with his men.

The Captain and his brothers riding to the palace to meet with the King

CHAPTER SEVEN

When Jack and his brothers arrived at the King's court, they were welcomed into the palace where the king was waiting patiently for them. King Marca had a feeling he knew what the Captain was going to ask, and he was delighted. He had been hoping the young captain would have asked him a while ago, he was so happy because he was fond of him. The King was upset about the whole mission and sad that his little girl was upset, but he had faith that the captain would return, which would make his daughter Maya happy. He had not even told her about the captain's visit but was confident she would be happy with the outcome.

This was the first time Jack felt nervous about meeting with the King. He wasn't sure of how he was going to start the conversation, but having his brothers with him made a big difference. As they walked into the King's office, the King stood up and welcomed them with open arms. This was confusing to Jack as it was not the usual protocol. When the

King returned to his seat, the brothers looked at each other perplexed, but they quickly bowed to the king who asked them to sit down.

After exchanging greetings, Jack worked up the courage to finally do what he had been wanting to do for weeks. He asked the King for permission to marry his daughter. Jack was surprised but delighted with the King's response. The King was ecstatic, and he also seemed relieved and more delighted than they were that he immediately gave them his permission for the captain to propose to the princess. Jack's brothers were all so relieved they shook the King's hand and hugged their little brother.

There was only one condition that the king placed on Jack, and this was that Jack had to return with the Golden Statue or at least to be seen to have tried to retrieve it. The king explained how he believed in the Captain and the men who served with him.

It was during this meeting that Jack found out about how the King was suspicious of his aid Jean Paul. The King was not sure what Jean Paul's intentions were, but he planned to find out. King Marca told Jack that he was pleased with his request for Maya's hand in marriage. He encouraged him to propose before he left as this would make his daughter happy. The King, with all his wisdom, had managed to sense Jean Paul's hostility towards him and his family. The King had his loyal servants keeping a close eye on him.

Princess Maya had locked herself in her room since she heard the news of Jack's departure. She was in tears and could not stop crying. How could her father do this? Didn't he want her to be happy? He had given his approval and he seemed happy she had finally found love. "This was all that Jean Paul's fault!" the princess thought to herself.

She was so sad that she curled up into a little ball on her bed and cuddled her favorite blanket that her grandmother had handmade for her. Would Jack be safe? Would he return safely to her or would he suffer the same fate the other sailors who had failed to return had? It would even be worse if he returned like the captains who had failed to reach the island of the skulls and returned empty-handed. The shame they all had felt for failing to succeed, most of them quit, and she did not want that for Jack. She knew how he loved his job. The princess buried her head in her pillow and sobbed. Maya was still crying that she didn't hear her mother come in. The queen had always kept extra keys for each of her daughters' rooms. She did not like imposing on them, but after she had been knocking endlessly with no response, she let herself in.

It broke her heart when she saw her daughter all curled up in a little ball sobbing. She went and cradled her and started whispering to her, "Don't worry baby! Everything is going to be okay." Unfortunately, the more she tried to calm the princess down, the more she cried. The Queen went down on her knees and instructed her daughter to do the same, she then began to pray. After they finished praying, the princess felt calmer, her mother hugged her, and this comforted her. Princess Maya looked up at her mother and she said.

"Mum, I am going to wait for Jack to return even if it means waiting forever. I love him and there is nothing and no one who is going to change that." The princess eventually fell asleep and woke up the next morning hopeful that her prayers had already been answered.

The King and Captain Sawyer discussing the
upcoming engagement and the King's
suspicions

CHAPTER EIGHT

On the morning of the Captain's departure, the men bid farewell to their families and boarded the ship. The captain stood at the dock waiting patiently for the princess. His heart was pounding in his chest. He was both nervous and excited at the same time. He couldn't wait for the princess to arrive. When he saw the royal carriage with its escorts, he became very nervous and breathless.

He could not remember the last time he had felt this way. He had never felt this way before. Jack watched the carriage slowly come to a halt. He couldn't move, his heart was now beating even faster, and he felt the butterflies in his stomach, and although he tried to move, he found it difficult to do so.

He looked over at his family who all smiled at him, his brothers gave him a thumbs up which made him laugh nervously. His men were all standing on the dock, all lined up to show support. Paddy was grinning at him and Jack shook his head and smiled. He had not pictured proposing to the princess in front of such a huge crowd, it did not help his nerves at all.

The princess couldn't wait to get out of the carriage. She forgot all about protocol and ran out of the carriage and leapt into Jack's arms. The princess was in tears. It made Jack feel hopeless. His father and brothers went up with him to show him their support. The King and his family were all present, both families stood around the captain and the princess, and they began to pray.

When they all had finished praying, the captain went down on one knee and took out the ring, he had been carrying around with him and proposed to the princess. Princess Maya could not believe what was happening. She screamed YES, and everyone cheered. The families, the crew men and the rest of the king's subjects who had gathered to bid farewell to the men, all celebrated the Captain and the Princess's engagement. Everyone was delighted, but also sad that the captain and his men had to leave. The captain bid farewell to his family and the princess. He reluctantly boarded the ship. The anchor was raised, and the ship Zahra slowly sailed away.

Captain Sawyer proposing to Princess Maya

CHAPTER NINE

As the ship began to sail, Raja, one of the ship's navigators, approached the captain who was with his four lieutenants. They were discussing what had happened before they set sail – they were all very happy that Jack was finally going to get married. Raja cleared his throat to speak,

"Excuse me, Captain."

"Oh yes, Raja, we have been waiting for you. What do you have for us?" enquired the captain.

"Sir, for us to reach the Island of the Skulls we will have to go across four seas before we reach the Island of Skulls," Raja responded.

Silence fell in the room. The four seas were dangerous. There had been reports of two-headed monsters and serpents and ships disappearing or being destroyed. Other things included mysterious whirlpools, waterfalls and so forth.

However, these were only just tales that were told and there was no proof that these things existed or happened.

These were the only seas they had never sailed across, and from the tales they had heard they were thought to have the worst obstacles anyone could imagine. Raja had worked with the Captain for years and was an expert at his job. He worked with a small team of men who helped him navigate and steer the ship away from danger, so Jack was not at all worried about these obstacles, he was more concerned about what would happen when they arrived at the island of the Skulls.

Jack turned and looked at his men who were all deep in thought and then he turned to Raja and said,

"Raja, I trust you and your crew have everything under control. I suggest you choose the safest possible routes that will ensure we all get back in one piece." Jack did not doubt his men. He had faith that they would be able to get to the Island. His main concern was what they would encounter whilst they were on the Island. No one had ever lived to tell of their encounters on the Island of the Skulls. There were only rumors but no real facts.

The ship had sailed for 10 days without the captain and his men encountering any trouble, but on the eleventh day things changed. They got caught up in a terrible storm. The sky became very dark and the ship had sailed into a very vicious storm. The ship was being rocked by strong winds that seemed to be blowing from all directions. The winds caused big waves that rocked the ship in such a way that all the men on board began to pray that the ship would not capsize.

The whole crew tried to secure the ship but struggled to stay safe. They lost some supplies including food and water.

The men were relieved and grateful to have survived the dangerous storm, so they prayed and thanked God for delivering them from the storm.

The ship sailed on but unfortunately, the little food and water remaining had to be rationed. After a few more days of sailing, they had run out of fresh clean water and food, five of the crew members had fallen ill, and the sun was scorching hot, which did not help. Jack did not know what to do except to pray, they did not know what type of illness this was, the ship's doctor had not encountered anything like this before.

Jack sat at his desk looking out at the clear sky, but he couldn't think of a solution. There was no telling how long it would take to get to the nearest island. Jack thought of the men on his ship; they were tired and hungry. The number of the sick crew kept rising. Jack felt helpless as a leader and captain of the ship. Pressure was mounting because everyone was waiting for their orders to come from him. For the first time in his life, Jack wished he was not captain. Paddy Wolfe walked in to find the captain deep in thought. He knew his friend very well, so he sat down to talk to him.

"Captain, I think we should consider turning back. Look around us, the situation is hopeless and the number of men falling ill keeps rising. We don't know what lies ahead and the men seem to be getting worse."

Jack cleared his throat and sighed, "Turning back is not an option, Paddy, we have our orders." Jack closed his eyes and made a fist. When he opened his eyes, he exhaled heavily. Looking at Paddy he said, "There is no point in us looking at the circumstances and letting them determine how we proceed. I have faith that we will reach land soon and the men will be fine."

Paddy smiled and said, "Then tell that to your face, Jack. You need to start believing in what you say. If you keep moping around with that look of hopelessness you are going to make the men lose morale and become even more helpless."

Paddy got up to leave, and stopped when the captain said, "Thanks Paddy."

"Anytime captain, anytime." He responded and closed the door behind him, leaving the captain alone. Jack thought about what and who they had all left behind, his beautiful fiancé, princess Maya, his parents, his friends and siblings. He remembered the tears the princesses and his mother shed as they bid him farewell. He looked at what surrounded him, the sadness and despair that filled the air. He looked at the situation and the circumstances the crew found themselves in, but then he remembered the mission. It was very important for him and his men to succeed. It was not just about him marrying the princess, but them completing the mission and returning what rightly belonged to their Kingdom.

He was not going to look at the negative things that were happening, they had come this far, and they had reached the first sea, so there was no looking back, and he was not going to. When Jack returned to the bridge, Paddy called all the men to attention, and the captain announced to them all to hear, "I know that things may seem bleak right now, and we are all beginning to lose hope, however let us not let fear set in, let us not let fear take over and stop us from succeeding and completing this mission. I believe that if we continue in hope and continue as we have always done in faith, we will soon be able to return to our kingdom and our loved ones victoriously. I urge everyone of us not to look at our circumstances, but instead we need to focus on what we are going to achieve.

Let's continue in faith and not fear, let us sail on in faith and not only by sight, because if we move by what we can see, then we have already failed, failed our king, failed ourselves and our loved ones. Now who is with me to carry on?" The men all stood up and cheered. Jack told his men to be on the lookout for land, they had sailed long enough without spotting any, he was sure something was going to come up.

The ship Zahra sailing in a horrible storm

CHAPTER TEN

Back in the kingdom of Aurora, princess Maya was restless. She had not heard anything from the captain or anything about his men and the ship. She was so worried she spent most of her time pacing up and down until one of her aunts encouraged her to fast and pray for the safe return of the Captain and his men.

Her friends also joined in on the fast and they all carried out prayer vigils as they believed that their prayers would be heard and answered. The princess, her sister and friends lit candles in the church every day and every night, and they vowed to continue to do so until the Captain and his men had returned safely. The wives and families of the crew also joined in. This soon spread throughout the whole kingdom. Everyone was fasting and praying for the Captain and his crew.

Princess Maya praying for the Captain and his
men

AS THE SHIP Zahra approached the first sea, the sky began to get dark and cloudy as if there was another storm brewing. Captain Jack and his second in command, Paddy Wolfe, told the crew to stay alert, according to the map, these were the waters of the Tsonga tribes. The Tsonga tribes were well known across the seas for their brutality towards foreigners who wandered into their territory. Rumors claimed that these people were uncivilised, uneducated, and some people feared they were cannibals.

The wind started to blow violently as the sky grew darker, but strangely enough, the one thing that the captain and his men noticed was how the water remained calm, they could not believe what was happening. The sky grew darker and darker, a few of the crew members lit the Masthead light so they could see ahead, the Sternlight so they were visible from behind and the sidelights so that the ship was visible from the sides. These lights allowed them to see any obstacles that could cause damage to the ship or put them in any danger, and they were also able to spot anyone or anything trying to attack them, so the ship continued to sail on. There was complete silence, not even birds could be heard chirping, and then one of the men on lookout duty called Seeker shouted,

"Captain the Tsonga are attacking!"

"All hands-on deck!" shouted the captain.

"Hold your fire", the Captain commanded, "We do not need to shed any blood, this could end peacefully, we are trespassing in their territory."

A few of the Tsonga warriors boarded the ship and fiercely challenged the men into fighting them, but Captain Sawyer got two of the crew members to raise the white flag, which symbolized their surrender. This was their way of letting the Tsonga know that they had come in peace and they were not a threat at all.

More Tsonga warriors boarded the ship, chanting a war cry known to many as the Tsonga battle cry. Captain Sawyer ordered his men to put their weapons down and instructed them not to make eye contact. The ship started slowing down and when the captain and the crew looked around, they were shocked to see the ship now surrounded by hundreds of small boats with four men in them, two canoeing and the other two aiming their spears, bows and arrows. Drums could be heard in the background and the chanting grew louder and louder as the ship came to a slow stop. One of the Tsonga men who seemed to be the leader, yelled something in Tsonga and every single one of the Tsonga warriors fell silent.

Jack and his men were in disbelief when this young man

began to speak in English, it shocked all of the crew members when he asked them who their leader was. Jack raised his hand without making eye contact, the Tsonga warrior approached him and said, "Tell your men to steer the ship and dock it near the island. Our chief would like to speak to you, captain." The captain did as he was asked. He could only take ten of his men with him.

Captain Sawyer and ten of his men were led to the Island of Chief Kayan the third on the small Tsonga boats and the rest of the crew men stayed on the ship under the watchful eye of the Tsonga warriors. They docked on land before they were led through a swamp. They had to cross a small river in the little boats that were docked at the river bank. when they got to the other side of the river bank, they found themselves walking through a forest, the trees were so thick the sun could not seep through, which made it cold and a bit dark.

Jack did not have any fear at all because he knew if the Tsonga wanted to kill them, they would have already been dead. The captain and his men could hear music, and as they walked towards an opening, the music grew louder, it was beautiful, soft music, which made the captain feel even more at ease. As they drew closer to the music, they could see light, and they could hear children's laughter. It sounded as if there were a lot of children about playing. This was confirmation to the captain of what he had thought at the beginning.

The Tsonga were not out to hurt them, he was curious though about what it was that they wanted. The captain was now hopeful that he could get aid for his men who were sick, it was such a relief that the Tsonga had found them.

As they made their way out of the forest they had to cover

their eyes because of the brightness they had to wait for their eyes to adjust to the light, and when this happened the captain and his men where breathless and stunned at what they saw, all they could do was just look in awe at the beautiful scenery around them. There were two separate waterfalls opposite each other with water splashing into a lake filled with clear blue water surrounded by many trees and flowers. The air was so fresh and clean, they were even more surprised with the beautiful log houses built around the lake and to the crew's amazement, the Tsonga seemed to be more civilized than they had expected.

The captain and his men were led through a pebble-paved street which led to a three-story mansion, which was heavily guarded, as they walked, the women and children lined up to see the strangers who had been brought to their land.

The Tsonga people were all dressed up in fashionable clothes, which was a complete opposite to how their Tsonga warriors were dressed. This was very confusing, as this did not explain why the warriors were dressed in such primitive attire, they had expected the people to be dressed the same.

Nothing made sense, everything they were seeing now was completely different to what they had heard about these people. The fact that they were all still alive was another contradiction to the many stories they had heard too. In the tales that were told, the Tsonga just killed anyone they encountered, they did not discuss anything with anyone, they were known to be a very brutal tribe.

Tsonga children playing

CHAPTER ELEVEN

As the captain and his men were led into the mansion, they were received by one of the chief's advisors and guards who took them to the Tsonga chief, Chief Kayan the Third, who seemed to have been expecting them, and amazingly enough, he too could speak English fluently.

"Captain Sawyer, will you and your men please join me for lunch?"

The captain looked at his men and noticed the looks on their faces, they had not had a decent meal in a while, and he had to admit he too was starving, but before he could sit down or allow his men to take their seats, he cleared his throat and said to the chief.

"Sir, I do not mean any disrespect, but I have men on my ship who are seriously ill, and they have not had any access to treatment. My staff on board have never encountered this illness and we were caught in a horrible storm which resulted in us losing all our supplies, so it would be wrong for us to sit here and eat whilst our colleagues starve."

The chief stopped pouring his wine and looked at the captain, smiling. "Captain, I have already arranged for your men to be taken care of, the illness you speak of is known as the red flu, we have already taken the medication and plenty of food to the ship. Now please take a seat."

The captain looked at his men and nodded, "Thank you, sir," they all sat down and waited for the chief to start eating. The captain and his men prayed first and began eating.

As they ate the Chief told the captain and his men that the ship Zahra had been spotted days before by the Tsonga scouts and Jack was shocked at how much information the Chief had about the ship and his men. the chief was also aware of all the trouble the captain and his men had experienced during the storm that had swept their region, but the Tsonga scouts had not engaged them because they were only a few of them. After all, they traveled in small groups and they did not want any trouble. Jack did not understand how they had not spotted these scouts, it was as if they had been invisible. The chief laughed when Jack said this to him and told him there were a lot of things, they did not know about the Tsonga tribes. Jack asked the chief why they had decided to engage them now, and was surprised by the chief's response,

"There was no way I would let you and your men starve Jack. I understand that this would be a surprise to you but don't believe all you hear about my people." He laughed and continued, "Besides, I have always wanted to meet the great captain Jack Sawyer, it is an honor." Jack was at a loss for words, he smiled and continued to eat.

The chief was curious to know what had brought the great captain and his men into their territory. The Captain narrated the whole story and the mission he and his men had to complete.

The chief ordered more supplies, fresh water and some medicine for the captain and his crew to be taken onto the ship. He then promised to inform the other Tsonga tribes of their journey through their territories so that they would not be stopped or harassed. Captain Sawyer told the chief he was amazed at how peaceful they were. The chief laughed and told him they were all a very peaceful people, all those things they had heard about the Tsonga were only just stories. The Tsonga did not mind because it meant they rarely had hostile visitors which kept their region safe and peaceful. Jack asked for permission to let their king know of how the Tsonga had helped him and his men, the chief gave him his permission to do so, and he also suggested the prospect of trade between the Tsonga and the people of Aurora. Jack liked this; their trip was proving to be fruitful.

After the supplies were loaded onto the ship, Jack and all his crew could stay, rest and recuperate. The following morning the chief promised them a feast when they returned from the Island of the Skulls. He promised to have gifts ready for the captain and his men to take back with them to their king and their loved ones. The Captain and his men bade farewell to their new-found friends and set sail deeper into the Kayan Sea. They came across a lot of different Tsonga tribes who waved and cheered them along, and some came close to the ship to give them food, medicine, water and other supplies, which they accepted gratefully. The crew members could not stop talking about what they had experienced and laughed at how they had feared the Tsonga because of the stories they had heard.

The Captain and a few crew members being
led through the Tsonga village

CHAPTER TWELVE

Back in Aurora, Jean-Paul was not happy with the women and the princess, each time he tried to approach her, her maids would get in the way or she would excuse herself or be too busy with her friends. The vigil for the captain, and his crew made him mad, but he could not help being happy, there had been no news, as far as he was concerned, no news meant good news. He was very confident that his plan was going to work out as he had always been good with strategy and everything was now falling into place.

He kept an eye on the princess even though she kept him at a distance. He never thought the captain would propose before leaving for his mission, if he had known he would have done everything in his power to sway the king and make him see how inappropriate this was. There were no guarantees that the captain would make it back at all. Jean Paul smiled to himself and marveled at how he was such a genius. He was going to have the princess' hand in marriage with her father's blessing,

He had worked it all out in his head to the point that he believed nothing would go wrong.

THE CAPTAIN and his crew sailed for a further two days and two nights after they had left the Tsonga people's territory. It was on the third day that they saw the most amazing thing. All around them the water was blue and so clear that they could see everything in the water around them. It was so beautiful, they all stopped their duties and stared into the ocean. They were all so distracted and talking about what they saw that they did not notice the gliders above them. As the gliders got closer and closer, the whole crew got more and more mesmerized and more distracted by the beautiful wonders they saw in the waters beneath them. It was as though they were under some form of hypnosis or some type of spell, even the great Captain could not help but watch the beautiful fish below. One of the crew noticed shadows, but before he could say anything, he was shot in the neck by a dart, making him wobble a little before falling to the ground. As the rest of the crew turned to look, they were all hit by small darts that made them fall unconscious.

When Jack opened his eyes, he found himself tied up in a chair, looking around, he saw three men standing in front of him. These men had what seemed to be like dark paint all over their bodies. They had belts with little bags containing darts tied around their waists. They carried pouches that contained arrows strapped on their backs. Jack cleared his throat to speak, he asked, "What is it that you want from us? We mean you no harm. We are just passing through." They turned to look at him and the man with the red paint under his eye walked towards the captain and said,

"Hello captain, I am sorry we had to do this to you, we had to make sure you would not attack, we too do not mean you any harm." The captain felt relieved. The leader went on to introduce himself to the captain. "My name is Kaytano, and I am from the land of the Chunga."

The Captain smiled and said, "It is very nice to meet you Kaytano, could you please untie me, these restraints are very uncomfortable." Kaytano quickly released the captain and commanded his men to release the captain's men.

Kaytano apologized to the captain and told him about the war going on between his people and their neighbours, the Chewa. He told the captain, his deputy and his Lieutenants about how the war started and how their wise men had told them about a great big ship called the Zahra, which would sail into their territory and help to bring peace into their land. The two lands could not take any more fighting; a lot of blood had already been shed. The captain was not happy about being tied up and getting shot at with little darts, but after discussing with his deputy and lieutenants, he agreed to do whatever they could do to help them within reason, they were not going to go to war, but would help to bring peace.

They docked their ship and followed Kaytano who took them to meet the rest of his people. As the captain and ten of his men walked through the war-torn area, they got to see firsthand the damage that the war had caused and the sadness on the people's faces. Unlike the Tsonga people, this was a very unhappy place. The children in this place did not play, laugh or sing. Instead of coming out to see the strangers who were walking on their streets, they all seemed to hide from the strangers who had been brought from the sea.

The captain and two of his Lieutenants were introduced to the leaders who were involved in the peacekeeping talks. Both the Chunga and the Chewa had called a cease fire after the ship Zahra had sailed into their territory. They all shared the same beliefs about the ship and believed it was a sign, so they were all ready to sit and carry on with the peace talks. To them the Ship was a sign from the heavens, it had been taught to them and passed down from generation to generation, the great ship Zahra would sail into their region and that meant the end of a long and unnecessary war which none of them could remember why and how it started, all they knew is that they hated each other and had to fight.

Captain Sawyer and his men remained neutral during the peace talks. They helped both the Chunga and the Chewa to start rebuilding their homes. What was difficult during the talks was getting the two Kings to come to an agreement that would help keep peace between both kingdoms. Both Kings were arrogant and prideful, which was one of the main contributing factors to why the war had gone on for such a very long time.

The two kings argued about everything, and this made the talks drag on longer than they should have. Captain Sawyer was a very patient man, but even he was beginning to lose his patience. They had to be a way for things to be worked out without the arguments. Kaytano, the young man who had spoken to the captain, could see how frustrated the Captain was, so he approached him and suggested something that he was sure would work and allow the peace talks to run smoothly.

The captain stopped to think a little and laughed at the

idea, although it was a bit strange, he decided he would try it out anyway. The talks were adjourned till the following day, both the captain, Kaytano and his men arranged for both kings to attend the following day, except this time it was without their advisors and servants. When the two kings entered the room, the talks were being held, they both noticed that it was just the two of them, the captain and a few armed guards. Both King Adamaya of the Chunga and King Ezra of the Chewa began to make a fuss because they both wanted their audience brought back in, the two kings even suggested that the captain was involved in an assassination attempt. If the captain had not got to know their characters, he would have taken offence, instead he concentrated on reassuring them.

Jack managed to reassure them and put their minds at ease. He guaranteed their safety and eventually he allowed each king to have one advisor present. They were all in agreement and, so they sat down to begin the peace talks. The talks seemed to be going smoothly until one of them said something that insulted the other and the peace talks had to stop once again for the day.

The following day, when both kings returned to the peace talks, they found a list of everything they had discussed documented, everything they had agreed to and what they could not agree on. Before they could start arguing about the things they kept disagreeing on, both their mothers barged in and asked to have a word with their sons. Both women did not look impressed at all. The queen mothers expressed their disappointment and they encouraged their sons to put an end to their bickering. They reminded them of how they used to be friends until their fathers found out and forced them to take over their horrible dispute that had managed to destroy their people's futures.

The two kings had taken over from their fathers, who had continued a deadly war that had been started by their great-grandfathers, which no one remembered why it had started. The war was just passed down from one generation to the next, and there was no need for the war to continue. Both mothers stayed present as the talks continued, and all agreements were signed. It was a good day for both kingdoms, there was going to be peace at last. The captain and his crew had stayed for almost eight weeks, which was a huge setback to their journey, but they were happy they had been able to help. The Captain never imagined they would ever be part of something as important as this. Both kings promised to reward the captain and his crew when they were making their journey back to Aurora.

Captain Sawyer and his crew meeting King Adamaya of the Chunga and King Ezra of the Chewa

AS THE CAPTAIN and his crew finally sailed off and continued their journey, they were all glad it was all over, they talked about everything that had happened and what they had managed to achieve and what they had been a part of. Some of the crew members had learnt how to use the darts the Chunga people had used on them too, which the captain and his lieutenants felt would come in handy one day in the future. The crew sailed for three days with no problems, even the sea was very calm. They only had two more regions to pass through before they got to the second sea. This would leave them with three more seas, which they had never sailed in, and the last one was where they would find the Island of the Skulls, in which they had no idea of what they were to expect.

BACK IN AURORA, Jean Paul spoke to the King about the captain and his crew, he asked how long they were willing to wait for the captain and how long he would want his daughter to wait for the captain. Jean Paul spoke to the king and reminded him that according to the law of the kingdom, if the princess was not married by age 25, she would have to have an arranged marriage. The princess walked in and interrupted Jean Paul.

"My 25th birthday is not any time soon, I am only 23. Besides, Jack will return way before that, I have faith and do not doubt that Jack and his men will be back."

Jean Paul responded by saying, "If you have not heard anything from the great captain by now, there is no point in even hoping he would come back."

"Enough Jean Paul! I will not have you speaking to my daughter in such a way, do not forget your place."

Jean Paul quickly looked down. "My apologies your majesty. I just wanted to highlight the facts, your majesty, My apologies again, sire."

"Will you just leave, right now!" the king bellowed.

Jean Paul left, and the king stayed with Princess Maya, reassuring her that everything would be fine.

Maya told her father that she would not marry someone she did not know, "Dad, there is no way I will marry a stranger, a man I do not know and do not love. I am going to wait for Jack. I believe he will return, and I do not doubt this. I have faith and I will continue to pray for his safe return."

CHAPTER THIRTEEN

As Captain Sawyer and his crew approached the third region, the crew stayed alert. They had not heard much about this region, so they were not sure about what to expect or what was to come. One of the ship's lookouts, Troy, who was one of the junior members of the team, spotted some people on a nearby shore and he also noticed that there was something wrong. He raised the alarm to alert the crew and then he made the captain aware of what was happening on the nearby shore.

The captain looked through Troy's telescope and saw what was happening. There was a big, giant creature in the water, this creature had two heads, eight huge tentacles, two arms, two legs with flippers, gills it used to breathe under the water, two huge noses under each big eye, and it could spit hot tar out of its two mouths. He also noticed that this creature was holding onto two men and it tried to drag both men into the water. The crowd, who were standing at the shore, were throwing stones and sticks at it, in a failing attempt to rescue the two men. The Captain put Troy's telescope down and turned to speak to Paddy and the four Lieutenants, Michael, Keith, Samuel and Keanu, but Paddy was the first one to speak.

"Listen up men, this has nothing to do with us, Captain, this will take us off course completely."

"Paddy, I understand what you are saying, but there is no way we can turn a blind eye and walk away from people who need our assistance." The captain said.

"Sir, it will make us fall behind even more, besides we don't even know what that creature is and how we can defeat it." Lieutenant Samuel said.

"I do know that we are to respect other people's religions and cultures but when a fellow human being's life is at risk do we just walk away without trying to help?" The captain asked.

Paddy and the Lieutenants all spoke in unison "No sir, that would not be right sir."

The captain then gave the command that the ship set course towards the shore. He ordered the men to target and open fire on the creature in the sea. The men opened fire, which caused the creature to turn its attention onto the ship. Although the monster was no longer fighting against the people on the shore, it still did not let go of its grip on the two men. It started spitting hot tar at the ship and the crew grabbed buckets of water, and they all tried to put the fires out that the burning tar had started. The creature's skin seemed to be like a protective armor, which none of the ammunition or weapons which were fired on it seemed to get through. The captain then instructed his lieutenants to help him look for a weak spot. The captain noticed that each head on the monster had one huge eye.

Captain Sawyer's right-hand men, Paddy, studied the creature and noticed it had some weak points, there were parts of its body that were not covered by scales. This was above the eyes, behind the gills and in the back where its tentacles emerged from. The captain instructed his men to target the weak areas on the creature's back, forcing it to release the two men, and charging towards the ship, the creature violently lashed out, causing a little damage to it. The men all fired at the creature, one of the crew members aimed above one of the eyes, which made the creature turn away and retreat.

The creature disappeared into the water shrieking in pain. The ship had been pulled to the mainland by the creature, which meant it had a few holes in it and had started taking in some water. The captain and crew got off the ship and tried to do all they could to salvage what they could before things got ruined by the sea water. The natives of this island were all very grateful and offered to help repair the ship. They offered shelter and food, which Captain Sawyer and his crew accepted.

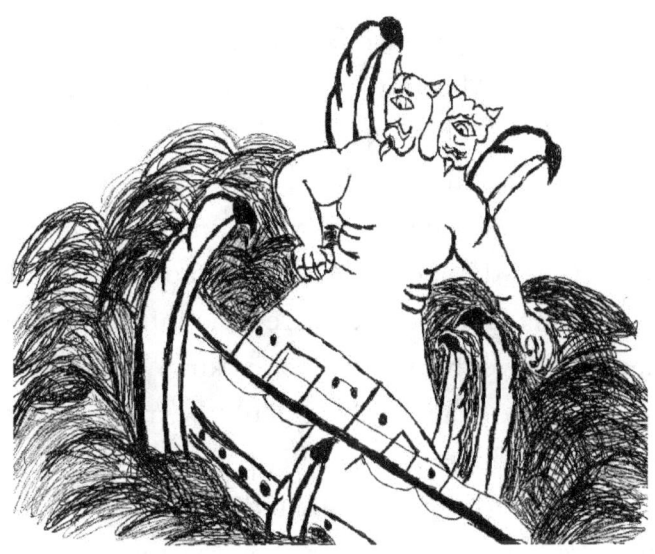

The creature attacking the ship Zahra

The captain and his men were driven in horse-drawn carriages and were taken to a beautiful kingdom, which they were awestruck by. The streets that led to the king's castle were paved with gold, the castle was huge, and the houses were all built the same, but they were still beautiful.

The kingdom had schools, churches and even clinics and a big hospital. The captain and his crew were summoned to the castle where the king, King Japha, invited them to stay as his guests. It was during this time they were taken to their rooms and were left alone to rest and prepare for the King's feast. The king wanted to thank them for their help in rescuing his son, Prince Erik, who was one of the men the monster captured. At the meal, the Captain learned that these people, the Nephee, who were a peaceful people, came under constant attack from this monster.

They did not know how to defeat it, even their army, which

was the best in the region, had failed, but after today they would be able to defeat it. The king promised the captain and his crew that he would help them repair their ship, and he would give them all the supplies they needed, food, water and weapons.

That evening the people heard the monster's howling. But what scared them the most was that it sounded more like two monsters howling. The people shared the information with the king's men who gave the message to the king. The king was very worried because he realized there could be more creatures and there was no way his army and his people could defeat these monsters. The king requested that the captain and his right-hand man, Paddy Wolfe, be present for the meeting in his private chambers, where he was speaking to his army generals.

The captain told the king what they had learned about the monster whilst fighting it. It was during this meeting that they devised a plan to get rid of both monsters once and for all. The whole kingdom was put under curfew and the gates to the kingdom were all closed and only the soldiers patrolling in pairs were walking the streets. The following day, during the early hours of the morning, they received reports from the men on guard who had spotted the monsters outside the city gates. This was a very strange situation because the monster had never been seen this close to the city, and for both these monsters to be wandering so close to the gates, they assumed that this was because they were out for revenge. After all, one of the monsters had been defeated the previous day. The plan was then set into motion, a few of the Captain's men and the Nephee men wearing camouflage hid in the surrounding forest and waited for the captain's signal.

The two monsters were still lurking outside looking for a

way to get into the city, when the captain and the army general set off an orange flare which signaled to the men waiting at the gate. The men got up and started firing at the monsters. This caused the monsters to slowly draw back towards the sea. The monsters began to growl and squeal loudly because they were in pain, and as they reached the area where the men were hiding in the forest, these men came out of hiding and started to fire at the monsters. The men all aimed at the weak points, which eventually killed the two creatures.

The Nephee had managed to defeat the two creatures that had terrorized them for years. The news about the victory spread and the whole kingdom came out to celebrate their victory. This was something they had not done in a long time. All they had done over the years was arrange memorials for all the people they had lost but, on this day, they were going to celebrate the victory. The neighbouring kingdoms had also lost a lot of their people, so when they had received the good news, they too celebrated the victory. The King from the neighboring kingdom, King Antonis, and his people joined King Japha in the celebration. When the captain and his crew got to see their ship, Zahra, they were devastated.

The two creatures had attacked the ship so badly that they could not see it ever sailing again. This was not a good thing, as it meant that they had failed their mission. The captain and his men felt hopeless, all they could do was stare at the wreckage in front of them. They were so devastated, and Jack had no words to say to his men. He just fell to his knees in shock. Jack debated with himself whether it was wrong to step in and do the right thing. He shook his head and looked at the ship. It was right for them to stop, and he would do it again, but it still hurt so much to see the ship in such a state. The men looked at each other and all that was written on their faces was defeat. It was over, they had failed their mission.

The two kings approached the captain and apologised about the trouble he and his men had to endure. They promised the captain and his men that their ship would be repaired and ready to sail within a few weeks. They were ordered to stay away from the shore, which they did.

Whilst patiently waiting, Jack and his men got to learn more about the people they had helped. They were not only wealthy, but they were a well-developed, intelligent, and humble group of people. The captain and his crew were fortunate enough to be taught how to make gadgets that would help them navigate the seas, purify the sea's salty water, and they would be able to take what they had learned back to their kingdom.

Jack missed the princess. He was going to do everything he could to get back to her. He believed and had faith. He never stopped praying. Prayer was what the crew did whilst they waited for their ship to be repaired. Praying was what helped them keep their hope alive, and it was what increased their faith, which kept them going.

The damaged ship Zahra

CHAPTER FOURTEEN

Back in the kingdom of Aurora, Jean-Paul received confirmation that no one had heard from the Captain and his crew, ships that had returned could not report any sightings of the ship Zahra. He knew the pirates were hot on Captain Sawyer's trail and they had also reported that they had not seen the ship Zahra yet. The captain of the pirate ship, Captain Brokel, intended to beat them to the Island of the Skulls.

He knew different short cuts to get there because all the pirates sailed different routes to the normal ships as they were wanted for crimes they had committed. Jean Paul was so happy he could not wait to hear news about the destruction of the ship Zahra and the demise of the captain and his crew. He had so much anger and hatred towards the royal family, he hated them with a passion. He had always wanted to be a part of their world, but unfortunately his weak family had been in service to the king. He hated that he came from such an unworthy bloodline. He hated that his family were sworn to serve the royal family, and the fact that he did not have a choice in it did not help at all. This was something he had not chosen but had inherited and every time he thought about it, it made him angry.

IN THE NEEPHEE KINGDOM, the two kings ordered food and supplies to be taken to the ship. The captain and his men were asked to prepare to leave so that they could continue with their mission. As they got to the shore, the captain and his men could not believe what they saw with their own eyes. The ship had been repaired in one month, and the last time they had seen the ship it was completely ruined. But to their amazement, the ship Zahra was ready to sail, it looked beautiful, brand new, and it now had a lot more sophisticated additional equipment and gadgets added to it.

The New and improved Ship Zahra with new
upgrades

THE SHIP LOOKED BIGGER, it was as if they had built a
brand-new ship. The crew members boarded their ship with
excitement, joy and laughter, they were all happy with what
they saw. The Captain was at a loss for words, his crew
celebrated, and they all thanked the two kings and their people
for keeping their promise to repair the ship. The ship was ready
to sail, the crew had been given a lot of supplies and weapons.
The two kings and their people had given the captain and his
crew a very good send off.

As the ship set sail, the captain could not help but feel
hopeful again. They were finally on track and were going to
complete their mission. The new additions that had been made
to the ship were amazing, they even discovered that the ship had

armor added to it. They noticed that the weak spots that they knew existed on the ship had been fortified, which made the ship a very strong vessel, the changes made Zahra a unique ship. They bid farewell to the people of the Neephee Kingdom and set sail to continue their journey.

They sailed for days and as they went past different kingdoms, they made sure they stayed as far away as they possibly could from the shores because they did not want any trouble. The ship had four crew members who were tasked with very important duties. Two of these men were nicknamed Script and Scribbler because of their gifts and their abilities.

Their jobs were to keep a written record to document everything that they encountered, saw, experienced and learnt. The other two men were called Sketch and Painter. These two were the ship's artists, they had to record everything in drawings, and the four of them were quite busy throughout the whole journey. There was so much they had encountered, and they also had so many new experiences.

The journey was well documented, the captain was amazed at how it all looked on paper. He got to look at a few of the records and everything was noted down from the moment the ship had set sail to that very moment. These records would be kept in the kingdom's archives and would eventually be added to the history books.

They sailed for two more months without any hostile or unusual encounters. As they were approaching the last region where the seas met, the water began to change, which made the ship start to rock and sway side to side. One of the ship's lookouts, whom they called Seaweed, noticed two whirlpools in the water, and not far ahead he noticed the change in the water, which was a sign that the ship was approaching a waterfall. He alerted the Captain to what he had spotted.

The captain ordered all hands on deck. With the ship's new upgrades and added technology, they managed to steer the ship and move it around the whirlpools, but as they got closer to the waterfall, the captain and his crew were not sure what to expect. The water current was so strong it caused the ship to speed up, and as they drew closer to the big waterfall, the Captain commanded the crew to get strapped in and asked them to brace themselves. He hoped that their weight would keep the ship from turning and landing upside down as it went down the waterfall.

The men started to pray and as they reached the edge of the waterfall, a strange phenomenon occurred. The water seemed to calm down, and instead of falling down the waterfall, the ship only seemed to move down to a lower level that seemed like a step in the sea. The ship started sailing again, the captain and his crew were all quite confused and amazed at what had just happened and what they had just witnessed. The crew members quickly snapped out of it as the captain bellowed, "Go back to your stations!"

They sailed for hours without seeing any islands or encountering any other ships. The ship's lookout, Seaweed, also noticed a bright light ahead of them. He sounded the alarm and pointed to what he could see. The Captain and his deputy were not sure of what to do. They could not go around the light and they did not know what to expect if they went through it. The crew members started praying and they also stayed alert. They were not afraid when they had encountered the waterfall, but this was different, and they all felt they had to pray because they did not want fear to creep in. After all, if it did, this would cause whatever enemy they might encounter to overcome them.

They were not going to let the fear of the unknown cause them to give up, turn back, or have any doubts and they were not going to let fear seep in and weaken their faith. They were not too sure of what was going on, this territory was a very strange place, so prayer was the only thing they knew they could count on and that it was the only thing that made sense.

The captain had two decisions he had to make. Either they continued to sail on, or they turned back and gave up on the whole mission. Captain Jack did not hesitate at all, he was going to stick to his orders and so his instructions to the men were to sail on. He believed that they would all be okay. The ship continued to sail into the light, but suddenly the light disappeared and then they were sailing into a horrible darkness. They continued to sail through the darkness for an hour. They could not see beyond the light they generated from the Masthead light, which allowed them to see ahead, and it enabled them to steer carefully away from any obstacles, ensuring that they did not crash into anything. Not only was it very dark, but there was a huge fog, and as they continued to sail, they started to hear noises from a distance. The captain instructed his crew to turn off the sidelights except for the Masthead light, they were using to light up the way.

As the ship continued to sail, the noises started to get closer and louder. As they sailed closer, the noises became louder and louder. The crew were all on high alert now and ready for battle even though they all had no idea what was happening or what was waiting for them. As the ship continued to sail, they began to see a small hint of light, and the fog started to fade away. As it began to become a little clearer, the noise they could hear was now much louder, which made it possible for them to make out what kind of noise it was they had been hearing the whole time. They had sailed into this strange phenomenon; it was the sound of war, they could hear gunfire and explosions. As they looked up at the sky, they were amazed by what they saw, they saw very strange flying machines in the sky. These things made a lot of noise and were firing at each other.

The captain ordered his men to stay alert. He realized that they had just sailed into a battle. Jack ordered his crew to put the ship's defenses up, which they did immediately as they did not want to be caught in the crossfire. As the battle continued to unfold in front of them, Jack noticed that his ship was four times the size of the other ships in front of him, which put his mind at ease, but he was not sure of the things he could see in the sky. The Captain would never take sides and did not want to get involved in whatever was going on. They had meddled in a lot of disputes already and there was no way he was going to lose his men in a battle he knew nothing about.

When it came to the people he loved, the captain would do whatever it took to defend them, even if this meant engaging in a full-out battle with these people he would. The ship continued to sail with all the men on the alert, they watched as the two sides battled, but the strange thing was no one got hurt and there was no damage caused to any of the ships or the flying gadgets in the sky. Jack found this to be very strange, they had not seen anything like this before, this was why sailing on was the best option.

Strange flying gadgets in the sky

CHAPTER FIFTEEN

As the two sides continued to battle, the crew on the Zahra looked on in amazement at the flying machines. The ships stopped firing at each other when they noticed the huge ship Zahra, even the flying machines stopped. They all turned and started to retreat. The captain and his crew watched as they retreated. The captain instructed his men to man their posts, "Full speed ahead, and let's stay alert!" the captain bellowed, "We are in new territory!" He shouted. The captain was not sure if the battling sides would all turn on them and start to fire on them.

The ship continued to sail and after thirty minutes of sailing they had to stop and were forced to drop their anchor. They were now blocked in by the battling ships and flying machines, except this time they seemed to be hundreds of them, and they were surrounding them from both sides. The captain assumed they had called a truce and had come together to face the Zahra and its crew. Jack quickly ordered his men not to do anything as he waited to see what these people were going to do next. The captain and his crew were asked to put their weapons down, and then they were told they were going to be boarded. Jack ordered his crew to cooperate.

Two small boats from each side, one red and one blue, cruised over to the ship and two army generals, General Ying and General Don, with two bodyguards each, boarded the ship and requested to speak to the person in charge. The captain asked Paddy Wolfe to accompany him to talk to the generals, and he instructed his lieutenants to take over and oversee the men and to be prepared for anything.

Paddy and the captain led the guests into the captain's office. It was in the office. General Don asked the captain,

"Who sent you to our land and what is it that you want?"

It was not often that they got visited by ships from the other side. They asked how many more were coming and why they had chosen to enter their region. The captain then asked both men to calm down as he began to explain to them why they had sailed into their region and he also reassured them that they had nothing to worry about, because they were only passing through, and he also told them what their destination was. The generals were not convinced, so they told the captain he had to prove to them that they were peaceful.

"And how do we do this?" asked the captain.

"If what you are saying is true you won't mind sailing towards the mainland." Said general Yang.

"Why do you want us to go to the mainland?" asked the Captain.

"So, you can meet our Kings." They both responded.

The captain agreed as this would prove that he and his men

were harmless. He asked to speak to his right-hand man Paddy Wolfe. After he had finished his conversation with Paddy and they had both come to an agreement, he told the generals that they would stay and meet the two Kings, and this was only to show these two sides that they meant them no harm.

The Captain and his crew were taken to the first palace where they met King Perto of the Tawana people and his wife Tamar. Jack and his men stayed in the Tawana Kingdom for four days. After the four days, they were taken to the other side to meet King Sena of the Bonda people.

It was during this time that they got to learn a lot about the two kingdoms and they also learned that what they had witnessed was not a battle but just a training exercise that the two kingdoms had every year as they prepared their armies for any unexpected battles or attacks from invaders. They learned that these two Kingdoms had come under attack several times from pirate ships and other Kingdoms. This was why they had made it impossible for anyone to find their way to them.

Both kingdoms stood and fought together side by side, and the only problems they had faced were caused by ships from the other side of the dark cloud. They had to defend themselves from a lot of pirate ships. The only reason they did not fire on the ship Zahra was because she did not look like a pirate ship. The two kings asked the captain to assign some of his men to their engineering departments because they were willing to share the plans to build the flying machines. The captain assigned this task to Mezzo, the ship's head engineer and his team of engineers. The Captain assigned a team of young crew members to learn how to fly the flying machines. Scribbler and the rest of the crew were assigned to keep records of everything they saw, they took pictures with the gadgets they had been given as gifts by the Bonda and the Tawana people.

In the fourth week, the captain put in a request asking the two kings to allow him and his men to continue their journey, He made a promise to them that he would use the same route on their way back from the island of the skulls. The two Kings permitted them to leave and warned them of a pirate ship that had been spotted using the northern side entry to the region by their spotters. It looked like it was headed in the same direction as them, it was going to the island of the skulls. They gave them a full description of the ship and gave the Captain and his Crew enough supplies and weapons. They wished them luck and gave them two flying machines to take with them. The captain was very grateful, and he thanked them for all their help. The captain and his crew bid farewell to the two kingdoms and sailed on.

Jack had a meeting with Paddy and his lieutenants, and it was in this meeting that the captain devised a plan and they also decided to be tactful about the last quarter of their mission. They were aware of the dangers they could face. The Captain instructed all his men to stay alert. The lieutenants discussed the strategy with the rest of the crew. The men rotated shifts so that they could all get enough rest. They sailed past different kingdoms and they all received a good welcome because King Perto and King Sena had told these kingdoms about the ship Zahra.

In each kingdom, they got to stay and rest and were also given new supplies, but they unfortunately received the same warning of a pirate ship being spotted going in the same direction. By the time they left the region, they had a rough idea of what to expect if they encountered the so-called pirate ship they were being warned about.

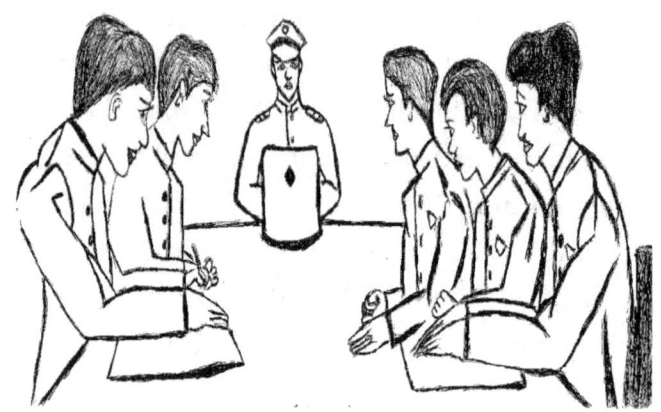

Captain Sawyer, his deputy Paddy Wolfe and
four Lieutenants in a meeting

Back in the Kingdom of Aurora, the princess kept having nightmares about the captain and his crew. She kept seeing the ship sailing into darkness away from her, and in her dream, she kept trying to catch up with the ship, which she couldn't do, and each time she woke up crying because the ship would have vanished into thin air.

Princess Maya was very troubled by these dreams, so she went to speak to her mother about them. Her mother tried to put her mind at ease, she knew her daughter was under a lot of stress, so she encouraged her to continue praying. The princess was so distressed, even though she was still fasting, and when she did have a meal, she was not eating much. Maya had lost a lot of weight. The royal family were all concerned about her, they all made sure one of them was at her side always, and if one of her friends was not there, her sister or mother stayed overnight with her in her room. They had always been protective of her, but this time it was because they saw the way Jean Paul had been trying to make advances on the princess, which was unheard of because she was still engaged to the captain.

Jean Paul had noticed how things had become different and he couldn't come within two feet of the princess without someone getting in his way. He sensed that he was being watched, at first, he thought it was him imagining it, but he did spot one of the King's men watching him. Jean Paul had been trying to put pressure on the king to allow him to marry the princess, but the King would not hear about it. This was not how he had planned it to be, everything was not working out the way he had thought it would.

He was the one meant to be standing by the princess, comforting her. He was confused at the family's behavior towards him. He sat in his office and thought about the whole thing. What was going on? He knew the captain was not coming back, he had made sure of that, so he decided to be patient. They would all soon come to him as the King's aid, and once the princess realized the captain was gone for good, he would then make his move again because the Captain was no longer a threat to him.

Jean Paul smiled to himself as he walked to his window, his smile soon disappeared as he looked outside, his window was facing the church, and just at that moment he saw the princess and her mother going in.

He was becoming very annoyed by the people in the Kingdom of Aurora and the prayer vigil they were having. It was almost a year now since they had last seen the Captain or heard about him and his crew. This was ridiculous, Jean Paul thought to himself. Why would they not stop? Why is it they did not cease to pray, even though they were not sure of what had become of the ship Zahra? They did not give up on their prayers and they kept their faith. Jean Paul just thought it was blind faith and they were all stupid to believe in any of it.

He walked back to his chair and then started to devise other plans just in case his plan failed. He couldn't help remembering his grandmother saying there was power in prayer. Jean Paul's father did not understand why he had turned out the way he had and kept reminding him of how disappointed he was in him.

KING MARCA SAT in his office speaking to his sons. They were all worried about Maya and they were debating whether to send more ships after the captain.

"Father, why don't you arrange a meeting with the commanders and then maybe after hearing what they have to say you will be able to make a decision." Prince Marca the third suggested.

"That is a good idea," said the king. "I will do just that, and maybe we can come up with a way forward."

The following day the King met with several commanders. They discussed the captain and his crew, and they all concluded that they would not risk sending another ship after the captain, not only was it very risky, but it was also expected that a mission to the island of skulls would take this long. With storms and unexpected obstacles, it was too soon to send anyone after them.

They would all meet up in a few months to reassess the situation. The king felt very low because he did not know how else to help his little girl. He prayed for her, the captain and his men every day and night and he wasn't going to stop.

The king could not understand why Jean Paul was so manipulative, conniving and malicious. He acted so different from the rest of his family. It was as if it was Jean Paul against the whole world. The king was beginning to think it was not a good idea to have Jean Paul in the castle at all, his family could be in danger. He decided to increase the security around the palace, but then he changed his mind about firing Jean-Paul because he knew there was something else going on and it would dishonour both families, there was no evidence yet, only just suspicion and a bad feeling each time Jean-Paul was around or tried to get close to his daughter.

He had not managed to figure out what Jean Paul was planning, but the King knew that whatever it was that Jean Paul was up to, it would soon be revealed and he would be able to get rid of him once and for all without creating an uproar in the Kingdom.

Until they uncovered what it was, it was better to keep him close.

The King deep in thought and praying

CHAPTER SIXTEEN

A s the ship Zahra entered the Kabula waters, everything seemed dead, even the colour of the sky was very different. It looked dark red. There were no birds in the sky, and the water was dark brown, looking in colour. The air smelt like dead fish and the sun was a dark blood red colour. There were a lot of old abandoned ships in the water and debris floating around. Jack was on full alert. He sensed danger, so he instructed his crew to stay alert and ordered the ship's armor to be put up. Jack couldn't believe they had managed to make it this far, his main concern was for his men, he was not sure what they were to expect when they arrived on the island, but he knew their prayers would keep them covered and protected, they would be safe.

Paddy stayed at the captain's side, everyone was alert and they all kept a watchful eye out. The ship sailed for another hour, but they could still not see anything. The air smelled very bad, it took a while for them to get used to breathing in the air around them.

It was after an hour of sailing that they began to see what looked like land, there it was, right in front of them, the island that they had been searching for. It was shaped like a skull and on it, to the captain's surprise, were trees and there was life on it. He was expecting to see vultures flying about, but instead there were different types of birds flying in the sky. The sun was now shining normally, and the sky was very clear and blue. When the captain and his men looked down at the water, it was no longer dirty but very clean and clear. The captain looked at his men and said,

"Alright men we need to stay alert at all times, we know what our mission is and by God's grace we will succeed."

"Yes, we will sir!" shouted the men.

The Island of the skull

The crew prepared themselves for battle. The captain ordered them to slow the ship down, and at the same time, they all kept an eye out for the pirate ship that they had been warned about. They sailed on towards the island but there was no sign of the pirate ship. Jack could feel a cool breeze blowing against his face, he breathed in and the air smelled fresh and clean. Jack could not understand why they had just sailed through that horrible scene they had just gone past, but he was not going to overthink it because they had finally arrived at their destination. He felt hopeful, they had made it this far and had had different experiences and encounters. He just prayed they would live to tell about them.

This was it! Jack ordered the crew to drop the ship's anchor, which caused the ship to come to a halt and with each man following their orders, the captain had three battle boats deployed into the water, and they set out and sailed towards the shore. Each boat carried six men, the captain sighed and looked back at the ship and the men who were left on board. He saluted, and they too did the same. Jack looked at the men on board with him and smiled. The other two boats were led by his two lieutenants, Keith and Michael. They were all dressed and ready for battle.

Paddy Wolfe was left in charge of the ship. He ordered the men on board to stay alert and to stay at their stations. Paddy said to his men,

"Let us pray for our colleagues as they go into the unknown. We pray that God protects them all and brings them back in one piece." Lieutenants Samuel and Keanu both nodded in agreement and the crew all said "Amen" in unison. This was it. The next time they set sail would be on their way back home.

Paddy had ordered the ship's armor to be raised as soon as the Captain and the crew had left for the island. They were all armed as they patiently waited for the men on the boats to reach the shore. They were also weary of any unexpected intruders and attackers who would try to board the ship.

As soon as Jack and the men reached the mainland, they all disembarked, and they hid their boats. They all huddled up and prayed, and then they went out in search of the lost treasure.

The three teams were equipped with gadgets they had received from the Kingdoms they had visited, so they used these to search and try to locate the missing treasure. Jack was quite impressed with this new equipment. It had managed to help them evade traps, quicksand and pits on the island. He now understood what his parents meant when they always said, "Everything happens for a reason." Everything that had happened and everyone they had met were meant to be.

If they had not encountered the mysterious obstacles and met the people they had met, they would not be able to evade all the traps they had evaded and navigating through this unknown territory would have been impossible. They also would not have received this specialized equipment. Jack sensed that they were being watched and as they ventured deep into the island the feeling kept getting stronger. The captain looked around, but he could not see anyone. Jack told his men, "Stay alert, men, I have a feeling we are not alone."

As they continued their search, they soon found themselves surrounded by pirates. Jack couldn't believe it. They were outnumbered. He shook his head. They had been expecting this, but he hadn't thought it would have happened so soon. Jack had assumed that the pirates would have waited for him and his men to find the treasure first. Jack realized they were dealing with a very impatient and overconfident group and so he signaled his men to stand down and not engage the pirates. He knew his plan would work. Both himself and his men had prepared for situations like this and Paddy and the rest of the crew were on standby.

The pirate's leader stepped forward and ordered them to surrender. He introduced himself as Captain Brokel and he also ordered them to continue with their search for the golden statue and the rest of the treasure. Jack and his men did not move immediately so Captain Brokel said to them,

"Don't be foolish, if you want to stay alive you need to do as I say."

Jack looked at his men, they all looked as angry as he felt. He was so angry it took all he had in him not to react. He knew he had to keep his cool. He needed to calm himself down, so he took a deep breath in and then he spoke directly to Captain Brokel.

"I am captain Jack Sawyer of the ship Zahra and we are from the Kingdom of Aurora." Before Jack could finish speaking, the Pirate captain interrupted him.

"Oh yes! We know who you are, and we have been expecting you Captain." Jack and his men exchanged looks as they were not surprised about what they heard. The pirate captain was well informed, and he seemed to know everything about the captain and his men. The pirate informed the captain that he was not going to let them go unless they co-operated with him. Jack closed his eyes because he could not stand to look at the pirate captain. He looked at his men and ordered them to do as they were told.

The pirate, Captain Brokel, and his men

Jack and his men continued to search for the missing treasure under the watchful eye of the pirates and their captain. Five hours later, after walking and searching under the scorching hot sun, they made a discovery. Buried under the sand was an old and very damaged pirate ship. Jack and his crew and a handful of pirates were made to dig for the treasure. After a few hours they eventually found the treasure they had been searching for. They all forgot about the circumstances they were under and started to celebrate what they had accomplished, even the pirates joined in the celebration, the long-lost treasure and the golden statue had finally been found.

Jack sighed with relief. They had managed to succeed. Jack and his men's celebration came to an end when the pirate captain fired a shot in the air. He told the captain and his men to move the treasure to where he instructed them to. It was after sunset that Jack and his men had finished moving the treasure from the old buried ship that they were tied up by the pirates.

The pirates began to drink, sing and were merry. They were all happy they had managed to get the treasure that had been searched for, for decades. During this time, Jack overheard the pirates talking about how Jean Paul had betrayed the captain and his crew. Jack was so disappointed. How could the King's aid arrange something like this? Jack began to worry about the King and his princess. Were they safe? The whole royal family was in danger. Jack tried to think of the reasons why Jean Paul would want him and his men not to return with the treasure but could not make any sense of it all. Jack closed his eyes and tried to calm himself down. He would return to Aurora no matter what!

Captain Brokel, like his men, had drunk a little too much alcohol, which made his judgment weak, and he had a boosted ego which made him even more overconfident. Brokel stumbled over to the captain and told him how he had some of his men take over the ship Zahra. He also told the captain that he did not plan on letting them go. He intended to kill Jack and his men at dawn, and the plan after that was to go and destroy the ship Zahra and everyone who was on it. Brokel laughed and said, "Jack, I am going to make you and every single one of your men walk the plank at dawn." He laughed again, turned and walked away before Jack could respond.

As the Pirates drank and celebrated, they did not notice the movements in the shadows. It was Captain Sawyer's men who had been left on the ship, they had been instructed to follow and search for the crew if they had not returned before sunset. What the pirate captain did not know was that his men had failed to take over the ship Zahra. They did not know of the new additions and changes that had been made to the ship, so when they attempted to board it, they were captured and imprisoned.

Jack and his men, who were tied up, knew what was going on, their colleagues had come to their rescue. The pirates who had been placed on guard were all dropping like flies as they were each shot by darts like the ones the Chunga had used on the captain and his men. The other Pirates were too drunk to even notice what was going on around them. When the captain's men attacked, the pirates had drunk so much that they could barely stay on their feet, so they were in no state to fight off Captain Sawyer's men.

Jack and his men were free. He was so upset and very disappointed in Jean Paul and his betrayal to both the king and the whole kingdom of Aurora. Jack just wanted to get back and so he ordered his men to take the pirates back to the ship Zahra. It was after they were locked up that he took Paddy and his four lieutenants to his office and told them what he had learned about the connection between the King's aid and the Pirates. He could see how shocked they all were. He too had felt the same way when he had discovered Jean Paul's betrayal.

Jack started to pace up and down in his office, he had to calm himself down, he was so worried about the princess and the rest of the royal family. They were all in danger and he had no way of knowing if they were okay or if Maya was safe. He could not understand why Jean Paul had orchestrated all of this and what he hoped it would achieve, but he knew he would have to confront him when he returned home. Jack knew he had to find a way to visit each kingdom they had promised to visit to maintain the new relationships they had forged on behalf of their King and kingdom, and they also still needed to get back to their kingdom in less than half the time it had taken them to get to the Island.

Paddy and the lieutenants all approached the captain and he suggested they leave for Aurora immediately. The other lieutenants were all in agreement, so Jack gave the order and the ship began to sail.

Captain Sawyer pacing up and down in his
office

CHAPTER SEVENTEEN

The trip back to Aurora seemed easier because the captain and his men had grown accustomed to the different regions they had entered. The Captain kept his word and they stopped at each kingdom that he had promised to stop at. They were given supplies and gifts they had been promised to take back to their King and their loved ones. It was when they had arrived in the Tsonga kingdom that the captain and the lieutenants agreed to send a couple of men in the flying machines they had been given. As Jack watched his men fly away, he hoped he was not too late. The plan was to get a message to the king. He hoped they were not too late.

Jack was grateful to all the leaders he had met. They had been so understanding when Jack had explained to them why he was so eager to return and why they could not stay longer. Jack looked at his calendar and realized that they had been away from home for almost a year. He sighed and looked out at the sea. He smiled at himself and thanked God because the weather had stayed good. They had not encountered any problems. They would be home soon.

Jack took a seat in his chair. He felt exhausted. Thinking back at what they had accomplished on this mission, they had set out with only one goal, and that goal was to retrieve the Golden Statue and the treasure, but instead they had also managed to make lasting friendships and had negotiated and arranged talks and trade between the new-found kingdoms and their kingdom. There was a lot they could learn and benefit from each other. They had managed to achieve quite a lot.

Jack was still concerned about his princess and her family. He was still trying to figure out what Jean Paul was planning but could not put his finger on it. What was Jean Paul hoping to accomplish? Jack and his men had tried but could not figure it out, so all they could do was hope and pray that the men they had sent in the flying machines had arrived safely and passed the message on to the King.

———

BACK IN THE kingdom of Aurora, Jean-Paul had got word from his trusted friends that some men from the ship Zahra had arrived in some strange flying contraptions and were meeting with the King. Jean Paul got very nervous. He did not like this at all. If the men who served under Captain Sawyer had returned, it meant that Captain Brokel had failed at what he had been tasked to do. Jean-Paul had already set a plan in case this happened. He quickly grabbed a few things and quickly left the castle. Everyone was too busy and curious to hear what was going on and what had happened to the rest of the men on the ship Zahra to notice Jean-Paul leaving.

Jean-Paul leaving

IT TOOK the Captain and his crew almost four months to get back to Aurora where they found the whole kingdom waiting for them. Jack was so happy when he saw the princess and his parents waiting for him. He noticed how thin she looked but was so overjoyed he did not fuss or focus on that. The good news was that she was okay, and everyone was okay too. Jack was so happy to see the relief in his mother's eyes. He looked back at his crew and they all got down on their knees to pray. They were so grateful that they had all returned safely, and when they found out that the men they had sent ahead had made it safely they all sighed with relief.

Everyone was home safely. The King had requested an audience with Jack and his second in command. When Jack and Paddy arrived at the castle they were quickly ushered into the king's office. It was here that they were informed that Jean Paul was gone, he had just disappeared. The king's men had searched the whole Kingdom and he was nowhere to be found.

The Pirates were taken to the palace where they were interrogated and officially placed under arrest by the King's police. The pirates were put in jail where they were going to wait until they were tried and sentenced for all the crimes they had committed against the captain, the King and the whole kingdom of Aurora. The treasure and the Golden Statue were returned to their rightful place in the Castle's treasure vault, which was where they rightfully belonged. The captain and his men were debriefed and they handed in all the records for every moment and all they had experienced during the trip. They handed in all that they had received, and they also shared everything they had learned. During this period, they were kept away from their loved ones. The whole process lasted a few weeks.

The Captain and his men were honored by the King and knighted for their bravery and loyalty to the King and the Kingdom of Aurora. The King made it official and gave Jack and the princess his blessing. Celebrations broke out throughout the kingdom as everyone celebrated the return of the ship, the captain and his crew, the returned treasure and the Captain's engagement to the princess.

After days of celebration and jubilation, the captain and the princess' family came together in agreement and discussed wedding arrangements. The date was set for both Jack and the princess to be married the following Spring.

Captain Sawyer and Princess Maya reunited

ABOUT THE AUTHOR

Talisha Antonio is a Zimbabwean-born, British author. She lives in Birmingham, UK with her four beautiful children. Talisha is the author of the Young Adults' and Children's book, Captain Jack Sawyer and the Golden Statue of Aurora, released in September 2019. Talisha is an Author of merit, having completed four writing courses, including poetry and screenwriting. Further, Talisha has published several articles in Flawless and She Inspires Magazines. Over and above this, Talisha won the 2015 PaWaR writing contest for a short story called Life is a Rollercoaster', published in PaWaR Magazine, page 23 (2015).

ALSO BY TALISHA ANTONIO

We are all a work in progress searching for a love that has no conditions. Discovery of our purpose in hopes of fulfilling our God-given destiny. It is during this quest of discovering 'Who I am', that Under Construction was birthed. Under Construction' is a collection of poems that reveal the different stages and seasons that were encountered. Each poem tells its own story and reveals a different phase or different stage in this quest for growth and a search for purpose. It is also

inspired by the different storms raging...Storms faced, storms endured and those storms that were overcome.